Naughty Spot! It's dinner time. Where can he be?

Is he
behind
the door?

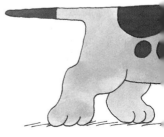

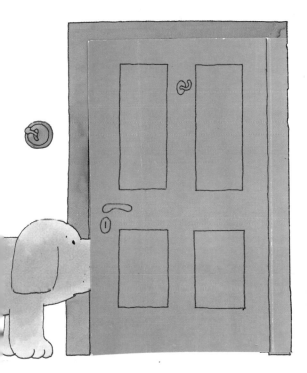

Is he
inside the
clock?

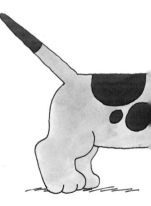

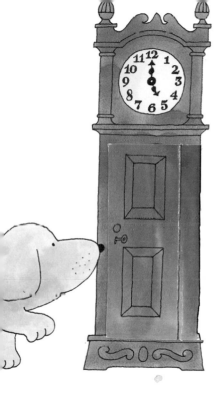
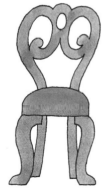

Is he
in the
piano?

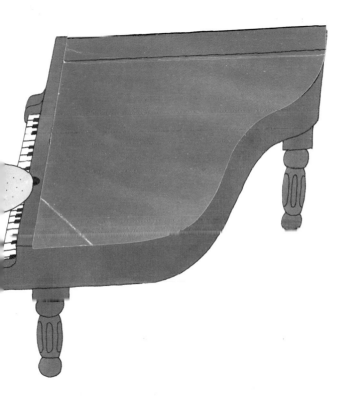

Is he
under the
stairs?

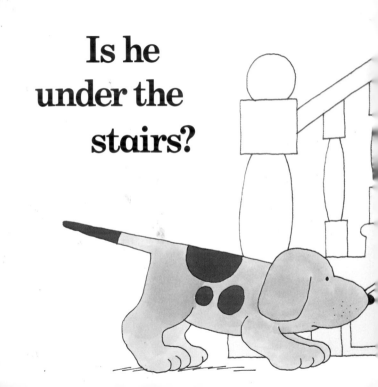

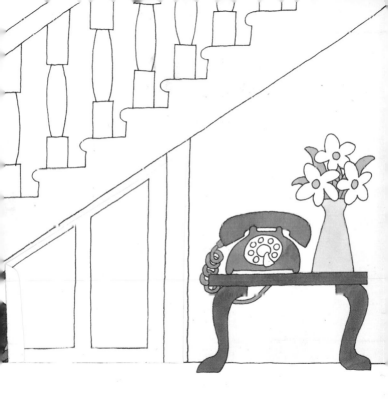

Is he
in the wardrobe?

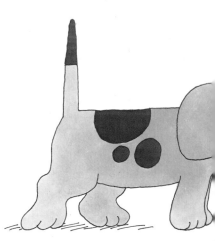

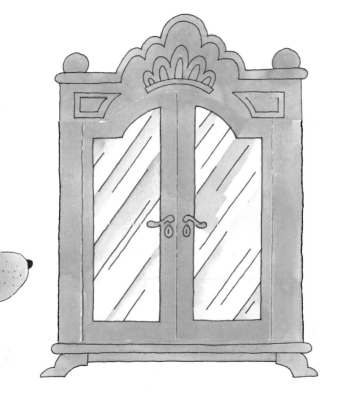

Is he under the bed?

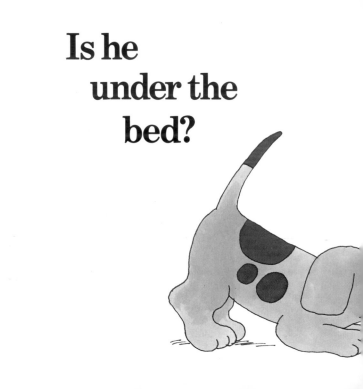

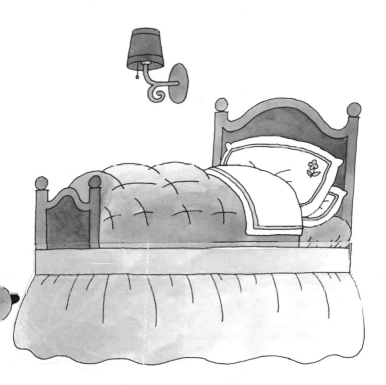

Is he
in the
box?

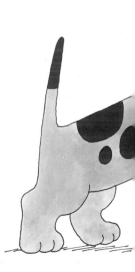

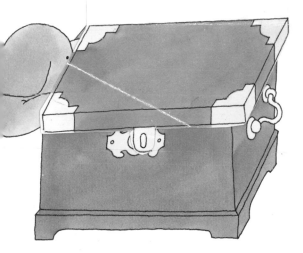

There's Spot!

He's under the rug.

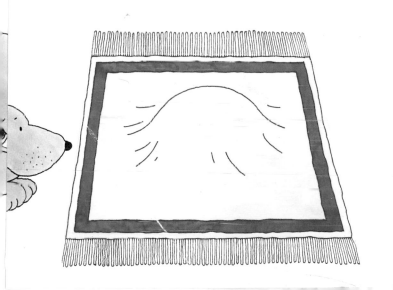

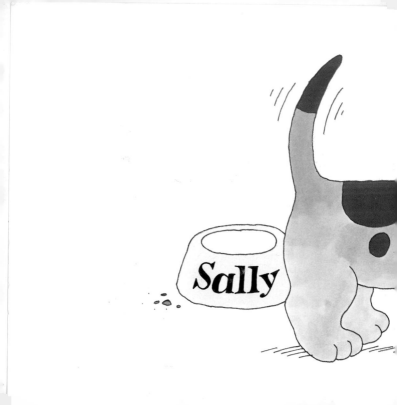